My Circle of Bears

My Circle of Bears

by Michele Durkson Clise

as told to Alf Collins
photographs by Marsha Burns

A Star & Elephant Book
The Green Tiger Press
1981

FOR
John Clise
AND
François & Julia Kissel
who helped start it all.

First Edition • First Printing
A Star & Elephant Book
The Green Tiger Press, La Jolla, California 92038
Paperbound ISBN 0-914676-65-2

Michele Clise shares her loft apartment and her life with 90 stuffed bears. Most of them are of an age and quality to be considered collectible. They sit on her chairs and desk, form a *corps de chambre* around her bed, and intertwine their lives with her own.

Their histories in the real world are mixed inextricably with their relationships with the other bears. The fact that Teddy Hawkes was bought at a garage sale from a stockbroker who thought he had outgrown his bear is just as much a part of Teddy as that he is infatuated with Alice and, at a party, is the kind of bear who jumps up and refills the teacups.

Michele gives equal dignity to what we think of as real and imaginary. Those who are relaxed enough to share this are richer for knowing the bears.

—*Alf Collins*

Moshe after hours at the Brasserie

Waiting for dessert

Introduction

The first reaction people have to the bears is to smile. A person who understands bears laughs, and then they begin a conversation—maybe not a direct person-to-bear conversation at first, but eventually. Most of my friends understand the bears. Perhaps it is a good way to select friends.

Because my bears are special to me, I created this book to see if the magical way that I see them could be caught in words and photographs, or if they would appear just to be bears that had once been children's toys.

One of the many charms of bears is that no two could be alike. Each bear has had a different owner, a different home, a different life. Some have been loved more than others, some have had better care, some have met misfortune but survived. Each is shaped by all events that have touched him. The changes of color and shape, how his face has sagged or his posture altered—all contribute to his developing personality. Some were cuddled and hugged and stroked. There are others who were loved but were dragged by a foot or an arm and clunked along behind. Some were operated on, some were mistreated, some were left outside in the weather. Some were set upon by moths or silverfish in an attic or basement, others were packed away in tissue paper and mothballs. But all my bears have survived and are still constant and loving.

Those bears who have been loved the most or neglected the most have the greatest appeal, just like humans. The personalities, affectations and roles that the bears take on grow as they fit in with other bears and as they meet people.

Sometimes accidents cause bears to develop whole new facets of their characters. Take Lily for example: since she was given a nurse's cap, she has taken to visiting sick friends.

Some bears are just stars—Lily and the Pope and Marcello have both personality and charisma, but Poli and Teddy, while they are older, are just nice bears. The quality of a bear has to do with being stuffed with straw or sawdust or kapok, and how it smells and with its worn spots. Part of the difference is good craftsmanship and materials. Bears being made today are like Barbie Dolls compared to old fashion-ed dolls. They are made of synthetics and plastic to make them safe and nonallergenic to be acceptable to a sanitary society. But they are inert matter and can't age with grace, or don't age at all.

There is a touch of sadness that endears bears to me, like layers of peeling paint on a beautiful old building. And there is a bear smell, musty, old and dry. It's the smell of an attic on a hot afternoon. Only good things that have lasted have that smell—trunks, and lace and blankets. It's a comforting smell.

Bears love to have fresh flowers and to be vacuumed, to smell pot-pourri and lemon oil. They love to be around when there's a party because they are usually included in the centerpiece and are always a topic of conversation for at least a moment or two.

One nice thing about bears is that they are not judgemental. They are approving, adoring, charming friends. They'll let you eat all the frosting off a cake.

Bears love to have parties with cookies and milk and tea and cakes. They love sorbet and meringues and chocolate, and they love it best of all late at night when we're in bed together—books and bears and all the treats. They love breakfast in bed, popovers, Dutch babies, honey and powdered sugar, and berries of all kinds. Bears love Château d'Yquem and dark chocolates, but they like jelly beans and marshmallows, too.

Bears are almost always funny and jolly and they like being part of the family even if they stand alone. They would be sad if their people put them away and never paid attention to them—or let them socialize only among themselves. When I think of them as a family, I worry about what would happen to them if something should happen to me.

The bears love to accompany me when I fly to Paris. They sit in the cabin with me, a jumble of them—and the cabin attendants and other passengers love to look at them and ask all about them. Sometimes they get their wings, sometimes extra candies and champagne.

We loved living in Paris because it was wonderful to make new friends. It seems to be almost universal for Teddies to provoke a smile and a fond remembrance of things past.

Sunday morning in bed for
Schnuffy, Zorba, Prince Albert and Anemone

Schnuffy

Schnuffy has done a lot of walking in his time and underpads peek out from underneath his tattered original footpads. He's sleepy looking and it's hard to tell if his eyes are even open half the time. He has a large worn spot on his rear, perhaps from a previous nervous owner or from having sat too close to the fire. He's very huggable because he's floppy, but he is also wise, comforting, steady, loving and discriminating—he dosen't like just anybody. He is a real Steiff and wears his original button in his ear proudly. It may be this sign of distinguished lineage that allows him to hit it off with Prince Albert and Anemone, both discriminating bears.

Schnuffy

Zorba, Moshe, Golda and Stella

Golda, Moshe, Zorba, and Stella all came from a collection in Portland, arriving with gold coins around their necks on ribbons. They were given their names here. The four are a family. Stella is bright and cheery and somewhat motherly. She bakes like a dream and her chocolate chip cookies are perfect. Golda and Moshe are inseparable. They like to sit off in a corner together and the other bears look up to them as examples of devotion, but they have never gotten much involved with the other bears. Zorba believes good will prevails in all things and is willing to live and let live. His sunny disposition inspires bears and people alike. All he asks is that the other bears do the best they can.

Moshe and Golda

Polar is a very large bear, as a matter of fact the biggest bear in the collection. He is white and he's not really a Teddy. He is a Steiff with mohair plush fur and stands five and a half feet high. He has chamois paws. He likes to wear a fringed shawl and sometimes he wears a white organdy apron and a bow tie when I'm having a party. He likes to think of himself as a combination nurse, butler and maid and tries to help at parties. He has very large hips and large feet and very large paws, so he's a little clumsy. Last Christmas he worked at Maximilien's Restaurant and it took two waiters' aprons to go around his waist. He stood by the wine and pastry table, but it made François and Julia, the owners, nervous because he was so clumsy. He had a red vest made for him by the designer of the opera and repertory theatre costumes. She said she'd make him a tuxedo. I don't know about a tuxedo for Polar, it might make him uppity. The other bears all like Polar because they think he is funny. Arfie, Glencora and Conrad always like to have the Swan Boat positioned near Polar. I am his foster mother because the children to whom he was given thought they outgrew him. I have a little thought in the back of my mind that someday one of the original girls will decide that she is not too old and want him back. Polar came to greet me on my return from Paris. I was surprised because it is hard to get him out of the apartment, although he does like to go downstairs to the restaurant on the hydraulic freight elevator. He has a little white bear, a Steiff also, that sits on his head, whose name is Conscience. Polar's a very impressive bear. You know if he could swing his arms fast enough there would be a big Whump!, but he can't. Maybe he needs to go on a diet or exercise, but it might change his disposition. We wouldn't want that.

Polar and Conscience with Arfie and Glencora

Prince Albert and Anemone
on Valentine's Day

*Prince Albert, Anemone and friend
on a Sunday afternoon at the Brasserie*

Anemone and Prince Albert are very pale and regal and fine featured and have a pale horse with faded pink wheels that's just their size. Anemone came with the Brighton group but met Prince Albert here, an obviously British bear of noble, if not royal, antecedents, and gave him her heart. Prince Albert has patrician features and a good, short furry coat. Anemone is tall and fine-featured, also. They are both gentle and sweet bears with lovely dispositions.

Sacha in his favorite chair

Sacha is probably a Russian Gypsy. He has a bellows music box inside him and plays sad, haunting, romantic tunes—nothing tinny. He is one of the shaggiest of the bears and has wonderful little patrician features, which suggest noble blood. He was probably one of the bears left behind from the excesses of Rasputin. Sacha sits by himself in a brown wooden chair, waiting, always waiting, for someone to come give him a squeeze so he can have music. He is somewhat selective about who squeezes him. Children squeeze too fast for the bellows. When children are around, he pretends he's dumb, like the rest of the bears. He had an arithmetic medal once, but he lost it.

Sacha

Clarence and Ophelia in their hammock

Clarence and Ophelia found each other quite late in life after coming here. Ophelia is probably in her 50s and was single until she met Clarence. She was bought at an antique show but no one remembers how Clarence came. It was love at first sight and now they spend most of their time together in a hammock. Ophelia keeps things stirred up among the other bears—she likes to keep things zippy. The British bears think she's dotty. She loves to pick on Lily and some care has to be taken to keep them apart. Clarence and Ophelia traveled to Paris by jumbo jet, and had their own seats. They had a splendid time visiting other apartments, particularly the home of a writer bear named Alvaro daSilva, who lives at 26 Rue de Fleuris, across from Gertrude Stein's house. Ophelia likes to put on airs about the French trip and drop little phrases now and then. Parisian slang. She is a natural blonde and likes flowers, lace, chocolates and per-

Ophelia packing for Paris

fumes. If she took a bath it would be a bubble bath. Clarence is a steadying influence and keeps Ophelia from stirring up too much trouble among the bears. He is quite literary, a good correspondent, and likes to observe life. He, too, is looking forward to going back to Paris, where there is lots to observe, even though it does make Ophelia a little giddy at times.

*Clafouti
Vanilla
and
Pepper*

Occasionally a new bear will enter the family. It does not happen often, but when it does we are all the happier for it.

Clafouti is a Parisian bear, found in a flea market on my last visit. I was with a Parisian who was delighted to have spotted the *"nounours"* first. It is very unusual to find a bear in Paris. Perhaps it is a reflection of the French character which does not usually discard or waste anything— and also a part of their strong sense of family.

Clafouti is named after a lovely fruit and cream tart. She is the color of cream and is very tall for a Teddy. Her face is rather square and her ears are more pointed than most bears. She wears a white embroidered cotton Edwardian child's cape and lace trimmed drawers. She also loves to wear paper doilies for hats and to carry French paper cornets filled with candies.

Clafouti has a friend, Vanilla, another white bear. The two are definitely meant to be together.

Clafouti in her finery

The British understand and love bears. They are not afraid to admit that they love them and are sentimental about them. Some of the bears are quite definitely British, or at least say they come from England.

Anemone, Brighton, Zenobia Onassis, Vita Sackville-West, Camille, Mr. Pyms and Prunella were bought as a group from a doll-and-bear museum in Brighton, England, and came here in suitcases. They left England as antiques and came in as old bears. Waiting for them to arrive was an exciting time, wondering what they would look like—like having adopted babies coming. All my friends were excited, they could hardly wait to come and see the bears. They have been somewhat cliqueish, except for Anemone, who has hit it off with Prince Albert.

Brighton fancies himself as looking quite bright and earnest but he isn't, really. He isn't very venturesome. He's a tall bear and has close-set but sincere eyes and can be seen to purse his lips sometimes. He's just one of those good looking kids who is always there but overlooked. At his own parties, guests keep coming up and introducing themselves because they don't remember him.

*A group of English Bears with Prunella,
Camille, Brighton, Mr. Pyms,
Vita Sackville-West and Zenobia Onassis*

Camille is the tallest of the Brighton bears. She prefers to stand, with just a hint of posturing. She has thick calves and may have taken a lot of ballet to get over feeling selfconscious about her height. It doesn't seem to have worked because her eyes are always downcast. She has recently been given a fur, jewels and a hat with a veil. She pretends that she's waiting for her lover, but I'm afraid it's just wishful thinking.

Camille

Zenobia Onassis has funny, thin legs and looks best in longer skirts or disco pants, which is quite fortunate because she is fond of tea dancing and discos. Some feel she dresses down so as not to show up the other Brighton bears, who are generally pretty dowdy. Her dancing hides a kind of shuffle one associates more with going down the hall in an old bathrobe carrying a toothbrush. She has made some quite direct allusions to being related to the Onassises, but her posture smacks more of the orphanage than the finishing school.

Zenobia improving her mind

Mr. Pyms is a retired civil servant who exists on meager service-related pensions. He may have a silver plate in his head from the Big War. He's sociable, but likes to visit humans rather than bears, because humans will listen to his war stories and buy him tea. If he's lucky, they'll buy him a little something to lace it with, too. He has a discreet drinking problem, which tells on his face. Unkind remarks have been made to Pyms by some who are not charitably disposed toward the elderly, the tired and the wounded.

Prunella has no looks and is left handed. She is always grumbling. She has a Palmer penmanship button and wants to find a secretarial position where they need a good, plain looking girl who won't up and get married and run off leaving them hanging. She came with a white duster cap and it is thought she might have been a Fleet Street char because she has been repawed. She has a tragic crush on Ernie Churchill and it is thought she used to discreetly look through his dossier when she worked on Fleet Street. She is very faithful and has a face somewhat like a gopher.

Ernie Churchill came from a London flea market and has all the trappings of responsible leadership—strong hips and legs that allow him to stand even in a wind. He has a worry crease on his forehead. His parentage shows. (He's thought to be an illegitimate bear of Winston's, no matter how hushed up it may have been.) He has been mended many times. Although he is worshipped from afar by Prunella, no one is sure if he even knows of it. He has a crush on Zenobia, who is reading *First Lessons in Beekeeping*, something Ernie has always wanted to take up in retirement. The other bears are charmed by the idea of his illegitimacy and would make V's if they had fingers.

Ernie Churchill thinking of past glories

Vita and friends

Vita dresses in purple because she thinks the Queen Mother does. Her dress and hat are purple but she would prefer true heliotrope. She has her own chair and loves to sit in gardens. Her lips are pinched, and she thinks other bears are frivolous, especially the American bears. She has made up her mind to put up with them to avoid class airs.

Lady Jane Padelford is almost an albino. She has the silkiest long hair but she's not vain. She's very ethereal. She wears a beautiful pink silk gown with a tucked empire bodice with blue ribbon bindings and beautiful little sleeves. It was made for her at Christmas time. She's a little vague and fey. She turns down invitations to tea parties because she says she can't find her long gloves. We don't know where she left them and think maybe she never had a pair. We all have our fantasies and hers is a pair of long kid gloves from Lanvin. She likes to sit near a bear-sized armoire, usually by herself, except at holidays when the bears wear their paper doily wings because they think they look like angels. Most bears have fantasies.

Lady Jane Padelford

*Toby
and
Cecelia*

Toby and Cecelia sit on top of my bedstead, always together, much to Toby's chagrin. He'd like to get away for at least one night, but she's always leaning on him. Cecelia looks much like a cat with her tail and pointy ears. I think she believes that if she just leans against Toby and keeps her ears down, no one will suspect she's not a bear. Both are pale blond, both shaggy and they're both small bears. Cecelia is very cute. Toby has leather paws and black button eyes and looks very serious. You see how sweet Toby is, he would never tell anyone that Cecelia looks like a cat—she's actually quite attractive, maybe even a little exotic, and he doesn't feel deprived. It's just that Toby is never alone. Sometimes it's necessary to be alone.

Spaghettini

Spaghettini is a southern Italian bear. A diamond in the rough. He had a scarf around his neck when he came but he lost it, perhaps he was taken advantage of like any other greenhorn. He is a good cook, particularly with pasta, and much admired for it by the other bears. His spaghetti is to the tooth and never gummy. He is a warm and generous bear who loves impromptu pasta parties. He strongly prefers white sauce, as opposed to tomato sauce, on pasta.

Violetta, Rosey and Garibaldi have a strong color affinity. Violetta is violet, Rosey is pink, and Garibaldi dark inky blue and they admire each other. Violetta is a fan of opera and things operatic and has a small collection of Enrico Caruso records. She likes to think of herself as a supernumerary in the opera of life and her name is always on the extra board in case she's needed. Perhaps she was a prize in a shooting gallery. Rosey has a prissy look on her face and takes care not to sit next to Violetta because she thinks the combination rather garish, although she would never say so. She is a fuzzy bear, which usually denotes a sunny disposition. She has a crush on Garibaldi, because she thinks his blue color may indicate blue blood. Garibaldi stands straight to emphasize his natural height and wears his medals and tassles with military bearing. He stands in a pale gray wicker chair with Violetta at his feet, much to Rosey's despair. Garibaldi has many service-connected decorations which he keeps around the house in drawers and teacups and saucers.

Violetta, Garibaldi and Rosey

The Pope came from St. Vincent de Paul thrift shop and has become slightly deranged about religion. He actually thinks he is Pope Vincent and it doesn't help that Marcello goes along with it. The Pope fancies that a pink stain on his stomach is part of a stigmata. He has a fondness for wine and crackers (particularly wine) and is happy to give communion to anyone who comes along. He has a splendid set of vestments and a wonderful buggy with a decal from Lourdes on it and a pair of leather gloves. He has been known to give and to attend some very decadent parties when he thinks no one will recognize him. When he takes off his vestments and his hat, he is just a silly little bear.

The Pope riding his Easter Rabbit

The Pope

Marcello is a blond, Northern Italian Bear. He has courtly manners and disposition and has been in the Roman diplomatic service. Before coming to the family, he had been to Tonopah, Nevada and Bakersfield, California, but didn't think much of them. He previously belonged to a lady with a fatal affliction who kept him on a cupboard shelf because her dog had chewed Marcello's feet, although Marcello had too much dignity to complain. He has small, rather weak eyes and wears trifocals although he tends to look over the top of them. His sartorial sense is impeccable and he looks splendid in his flowing, old fashioned, black silk bow tie. His real passion is the piano and he expends much scholarly research in seeking the lost chord. His paw span of three keys is the envy of visiting bear musicians. He likes Ravel and plays classical music well. Left handed concertos are his forte. He spends quite some time with the Pope, but is not quite sure how much of the Pope's delusion to take seriously. He has, after all, been promised a Papal Ambassadorship shortly. He is always deferential to the Pope and they like to go carousing every once in awhile.

Marcello searching for the lost chord

Moussaka and friends

Moussaka

Moussaka is a Greek bear with a wonderful wooden mouth that goes clickety click. He's sort of a cinnamon color with vivid eyes and a distinct nose. He's not like any of the other Teddies. He's a regal bear, always smiling, and has a chaise he loves to sit on. He has a secret crush on Zenobia but she won't have anything to do with him because they are both Greek and he's old hat to her. He talks a lot and usually can be found drinking retsina or turkish coffee. He has great long arms and he always makes me smile because he looks like he just stopped doing something.

39

Nicolaus and Ricky Jaune, Rosita, Edwardo and Juan Miguel and Aurora

Boris and his heart collection

Boris is a dark brown bear—small, with a very intense looking face. He is very serious and I always like to have him near a bouquet of flowers in the bedroom. He has a small collection of hearts and is especially fond of chocolate hearts and Valentine's Day.

Brady Boeing is a distant cousin of Amanda Rose Boeing. They don't look anything like each other. He's dark brown, has short hair, a patch on one eye, and an arm in a sling. He came that way and has never bothered to explain what happened. The other bears are very discreet and don't press the question. Brady is portly and likes to sit around the club. He doesn't say a lot, he doesn't have much personality.

Oscar from Ballard has soakers and wants to go to Alki Beach. The soakers are at half mast and he'll never get there like that. He has a wonderful old-bear smell.

Barney is one of the early bears in the family, coming from the Salvation Army for five dollars, which was a lot, then. He was in a toy barrel. He's a taupe velour in very firm shape and quite distinguished. He worked in a real estate office at the Pike Place Market for quite some time and many letters went out countersigned by him. He has a striking presence. Part of his office work was acting as nightwatchman and it is rumored that he is rated black belt in judo. Now that he's retired, he wants to rest. He usually sprawls by himself because he's in his Golden Years. He's well regarded in the family and gets along with everybody.

Brady Boeing, Boris, Oscar and Barney

Arfie and Glencora sit in the Swan Boat and together they cut quite a figure. Arfie wears a dress and a gray hat with a pink rose. Although Conrad doesn't give the slightest hint, it is said that he really covets the hat. Arfie likes to stand on the heat register when he is out of the Swan Boat until his dress and hat are quite soiled, but it is all for comic effect. He is the funniest of the bears and fits in with any crowd. His puns make all the other bears growl and his growls are infectious. There used to be a poodle dog in the family that would come over and single him out for a good shaking, but the dog went away. Glencora is about 45 years old and is pretty if somewhat vacuous. She's the kind of girl who looks great in hats and dresses and loves ruffles and Arfie. She tries to sit still no matter how much the Swan Boat rocks. She's Irish but not too bright and has an organdy dress and a hat.

Arfie and Glencora in the Swanboat

Arfie, Glencora and Conrad

Conrad

Conrad is a pale gray bear with wonderful gray and black eyes. There are some who think Conrad is a sissy just because he wears an organdy christening dress. He wears it because it looks becoming on him. He also wears a ribbon with French roses on it, but he's not afraid of that. He's his own bear. He's climbed mountains, he's travelled, he knows fine foods and wine. He loves to sit on a white daybed because it's artistic. He likes to be near Arfie and Glencora because they have similar tastes in clothing. Although he has a rather bleak look with his bare forehead, he is quite self-confident and outgoing.

Posey has a very round face, and funny little ears. She's yellow. Her name is Posey because her mouth says "Pooooooosey". She loves flowers and likes to wear a little straw hat with ribbons and an elastic under the chin. Posey would really love to have a navy blue pleated skirt, a white middy, high white socks and black Mary Janes. Hopefully a doll her size will come along with just this sort of outfit. Until then, she's happy to sit by the flowers, especially geraniums, salmon-pink ones. She also likes Sonia roses and apricots. She is a loner, an old bear, 50 or 60 years old, and likes the prerogatives of old age. Lots of the bears are good natured, but most are loners. They stay off by themselves or in a little group, yet they have natural spots where they seem to fit.

Posey with Bernie and Doggie

Lily is a tall brunette. When she arrived, she was the most expensive bear we ever had, and never lets anyone forget it. She is somewhat of a social climber and thinks that her price tag has something to do with being a superior person. She thinks none of the other bears are good enough and she's always searching for richer and more attractive bears. She sits alone in her carriage and has an extensive wardrobe—an ermine scarf, a white fur coat, a fur muff, lots of organdy dresses, a pink Jean Harlow nightgown, a black taffeta cape and muff and lots of hats. She has a watch. She and Ophelia compete. Lily never lets Ophelia forget when she wore a dirty dress and a curler in her hair. Lily says Ophelia is not a natural blonde. They tease unmercifully and because of her airs, Lily usually comes off second best. Lily is about 60 human years old and of American descent. She was spoiled by her human father. The thought of a new dress or coat will keep her going happily for days.

Lily

Portrait of Lily

Alex and his tiny friends

Alex is a tiny bear. He's named after an orange tiger cat. He sits in a grand little frieze chair, just his size, which is one of the things that makes it so nice. Lily and Ophelia get a little nitty about it at times but basically bears are constant friends. I don't know that Alex thinks a lot, he just sits in his chair at the base of a lamp. He likes it best when the lamp is on because that means it's nighttime, when everyone is home.

Faux Bear has a face similar to a monkey, but I am sure he is a bear and so is he. His poor little feet are tattered and torn, but he does not want to submit to a pawdectomy, even though he will feel better after its done. He has a bellows music box in his chest. We did not discover this until he had lived in our house for several years. He was very pleased for us to discover this hidden talent.

Faux Bear

Amanda Rose Boeing is a blonde with big loppy, square ears and rose pink eyes. She's of medium height and straight up and down—she doesn't have any hips. She's a pleasant bear and there's something about her that always makes me smile. When one addresses her, one always says her full name, even the other bears always say "Amanda Rose Boeing", because there is a certain air about it. She likes it. Alice particularly likes to say "Amanda Rose Boeing" and so does Ernie Churchill, because he likes the sound of the English language. Amanda Rose Boeing stands next to Schnuffy and the rest of the yellow bears, because she has a great sense of color, possibly because her name has color in it.

Amanda Rose Boeing

Martin is a splendid bear who is 65 years old. I saw a picture of his former mother when she was a child with Martin in her hand. He has a splendid apple green and white romper suit, the kind with the top that buttons to the bottom, with Peter Pan collar and cuffs. He has a black cowboy hat and a cap pistol tucked into his waist band. He rides a nice horse—a Steiff named Horsey. Actually, it's not a horse, it's a pony on wheels. Martin rides him sort of sidesaddle because he has trouble sitting on Horsey well. Sometimes Martin sits downstairs in the restaurant and when he does, the maitre d' and the waiters just roll their eyes. They've told him it's impolite to wear his hat in a French restaurant, but Martin just says he's from western France. Martin thinks of himself as being kind of tough. It's hard to believe when he wears his sissy suit. He has another romper suit with mulberry collar, cuffs and pants but he thinks the green is more becoming. He is not really tough.

Martin and Horsey

It is difficult to tell one of the Nigels from another, not so much because they look alike, but because they have the same lack of personality. They try to arrive at parties separately because it is embarrasing for acquaintances to continually get them mixed up.

One of the Nigels is quite tall, one has a pronounced long nose and the other wears maroon knit soaker overalls. When that Nigel gets fed up with being confused with the others, he wears his soakers as a cape, crossing the straps across his chest, and calling himself Captain Nigel. As a trio they have quite a bit of substance and no one knows why they shouldn't be more memorable. Perhaps it's because they haven't any bare patches from being loved. But they really can't help that.

Walla, Walla and Zillah are twins with a close cousin. When they came from east of the mountains, they were wearing knickerbockers. They are rather rustic. They were made in the '20s and are chocolate brown, furry, with brown velvet paws and snouts and flat faces. You can tell Walla from Walla because he has a bad eye—a broken button. They are funny because they like to say "Walla Walla and Zillah".

The three Nigels, Walla, Walla and Zillah

Bertie was found in a box brought down from an attic. He was wearing some rather ratty high button shoes, which he quickly kicked off. He also had some rather suspicious appearing stuffing and went right to the fumigator. He had a growler, which is gone, and has had a total spinal fusion, a triple pawdectomy and a mouth relocation, above his nose. Even so, he does have a certain something about him, a touch of nobility. He is thought to be British, although no one can be certain and he doesn't associate with the British bears. He stands in a corner, leaning against a pillow to favor the fusion and thinking about the box in the attic where no one bothered him. The other bears tease him, always saying that they hear buzzing around him. It's not hard for him to keep a stiff upper lip, however.

Bertie

Mona and Jello came at different times from second hand shops at the Pike Place Market.

Mona, left to her own devices, would be one of those bears you see along the streets, sorting through the trash cans for valuables. Her taste in clothes runs to the bizarre and she likes to wear socks for gloves, which is okay because a bear's hands don't look much different from their feet anyway. Mona sits quietly with her nose in the air and the enigmatic smile which gives her her name. She wears a paper flower in her bosom and carries a lace handkerchief in it. Her worn hands show a life of hard work and she knows she has a good thing going for her now. She certainly isn't frivolous. She is probably American. Jello is nubby yellow all over, a stocky, compact fellow who is always smiling and in a good humour. He was probably owned by a happy child. He tends to talk too much and he worries about moths and termites (a bear's natural enemies). The greatest thing that ever happened to him was that a woodcarver used him as a model for a wooden bear. Jello thinks the likeness quite remarkable.

Mona with Jello and his after-image

Alcibiades is a widely traveled classicist. He was picked up by his first mother at the factory in Denver in 1904 and then matriculated at Mount Holyoke College, class of '21. He spent 33 years in China, where he picked up acupuncture and, for some unaccountable reason, voodoo. He has an assortment of pins and needles and does pawdectomies. The other bears stay away from him because a bear will let his stuffing fall out before he'll submit to a pawdectomy. Alcibiades came dressed in worker blue overalls and a red sash around his neck and is thought to have had something to do with the coming to power of the present Chinese government. He is unwilling to talk much about his experiences "behind the Great Wall" except to say "in China it's all different." But he won't say how. He likes to go to Chinese restaurants and gets the rice bowl right up to his mouth. He prides himself on being "a bear ahead of his time" in graduating from a woman's college and having been in China at the time of the Great March. He always has been a bit of an individualist. He has longer arms and a more pronounced hump than most bears and is stuffed with cotton.

Alcibiades

Poli and Teddy are both members of the first shipment of real Teddy bears to Seattle in 1903. Both stayed in the same family with their original owner, until coming here to me. Both are well-preserved German Steiffs. Poli has squeezing problems with his waist stuffing. He was in the basement for quite some time and lost much of his zip. He doesn't have much personality. Teddy has more stuffing left than Poli and is a little bit smarter and has more persona. Poli likes to be introduced as "Seattle's first Teddy bear." He thinks that makes him better than the other bears whereas it just makes him older. It grates on Teddy a little bit. Nevertheless, they are inseparable and care nicely for each other.

Poli and Teddy in their garden

Theodore

Theodore has a large clock hanging around his neck. He is sometimes mistaken for a bear with a clock in his stomach, but he's not. He's very precise and demanding, probably a German bear, but not a Steiff. Maybe he's Swiss. He is a good, proper brown color. He feels he is the only bear worth his salt because he works very hard keeping time and helping the bears and me to keep appointments.

Vita, Teddy, Poli, Albert, Anemone and Schnuffy

Many of the bears love to go to restaurants after hours. They prefer the later hours or Sunday afternoons when their favorite restaurants are closed because they are really quite shy outside their own intimate circle.

Teddy Hawkes and Alice are bon vivants in bear circles. Alice is sought after as a party guest by both Lily and Ophelia because she is *tres amusant*. She hasn't travelled much but she reads the New Yorker and is a wealth of information in a witty, polished sort of way. Teddy Hawkes sits on quilts and really doesn't care about anything else but going to parties with Alice. He's the kind that jumps up and refills the teacups and he's always saying things like, "Tell them about this week's 'Talk of the Town,' Alice". No one is at all certain where Alice came from. Except for her manufacturer's tag, you would think she is homemade because she is so haphazard looking. Her body is a loosely woven fabric. She has a leather collar sewn on and a lot of work has been done on her including a fuchsia lipstick mouth of wool felt. She wears a pince nez on a black ribbon and is named for Alice Longworth Roosevelt. She is one of those funny ladies with runny lipstick who never blots it and leaves big smears on tea cups but otherwise is a perfect guest. She likes everyone and gets along with everyone and her humor is never at anyone's expense. Teddy Hawkes came from an estate sale in a house where he had lived for 50 years. He belonged to a lad who became a stockbroker and thought he outgrew his bear. Teddy used to be golden. He has been to a couture shop three times where they have tried to copy him for a pattern, without success. He is a gentle, sociable fellow who is truly in love with Alice, and Alice knows a good thing when she sees it and is very kind to Teddy Hawkes.

Teddy Hawkes and Alice Longworth Roosevelt

I wish to extend my special thanks to:
Karen Bell, Alf and Shirley Collins, Michael and Marsha Burns,
Leroy and Joie Soper, Patrick Soden, Tom Orton, Louise and Gary
Drager, Bruce Guenther, Ed Marquand, Camille and Luther
McLean, Roberta and Ernie Sherman, Sandra and Harold Darling,
Richard T. Nelson, David Marshall, George Hamilton, Lou and
Sara Nawrot, Patsy Ballard, the staff of Brasserie Pittsbourgh, Max-
imilien's, the City Loan Pavillon, the Elliot Bay Book Company and
Cafe, and all the Bears and friends too numerous to mention here.
—*Michele Durkson Clise*

The text of this book was set in Goudy Old Style, at Torrey Services, San Diego.
Titles set in Snell Roundhand.
Captions hand lettered by Judythe Sieck.
The color separations and black & white halftones were made
by Photolitho, AG., Zurich Switzerland.
Stripping & press preparation by Darian Powell.
Printing by Albert Hutchins
at The Green Tiger Press.